I've Got
Bunny Business!

Dear Michelle,

My best friend
gave me a parrot
for my birthday.
It's really cool
and it even talks!
But every time I
go near the
cage I sneeze
like crazy. How
can I give away
my bird without
hurting my
friend's feelings?

Yours truly,
Bird Trouble

Dear Michelle,
I made a big mistake.
Last week during recess
I ate a banana on top of
the monkey bars. Now
everybody calls me
monkey brains!!! How
do I get them to
stop?

Sincerely,
Not a Monkey

Dear Michelle,
My mom says that when I grow up I
can be anything I want to be. Well, I
want to be a turtle. I told my brother
this and he laughed at me. What's
so wrong with turtles?
From
Slow and Steady Wins the Rac

I've Got
Bunny Business!

by Katherine Noll and Tracey West

📚HarperEntertainment
An Imprint of HarperCollins*Publishers*

A PARACHUTE PRESS BOOK

A PARACHUTE PRESS BOOK

Parachute Publishing, L.L.C.
156 Fifth Avenue
Suite 302
New York, NY 10010

Published by
≜HarperEntertainment

An Imprint of HarperCollins*Publishers*
10 East 53rd Street, New York, NY 10022-5299

ISBN 0-06-054086-9

HarperCollins®, ≜® , and HarperEntertainment™ are trademarks of
HarperCollins Publishers Inc.

First printing: March 2004

Printed in the United States of America

Visit HarperEntertainment on the World Wide Web at
www.harpercollins.com

10 9 8 7 6 5 4 3 2 1

Chapter One

"Chocolate bunnies! That's my favorite part of Easter," I told my two best friends, Cassie Wilkins and Mandy Metz.

It was Monday afternoon. Spring vacation was only a week away—and so was Easter! And the kids in my third-grade class were making cute bunny masks out of paper plates.

"I love chocolate bunnies too," Cassie said. "Especially the ears. I always bite those off first!"

Mandy grabbed the blue bunny mask she had painted. She held it in front of her face. "Owwwww! Please don't eat my ears!" she said in a squeaky voice.

Cassie and I both laughed.

"Don't forget to cut out the eye holes in your masks," Mrs. Ramirez reminded us. She walked around the room, checking out everybody's art. She stopped by my desk. "That's a pretty yellow bunny, Michelle," she told me.

I smiled. Mrs. R. has to be the nicest teacher at Fraser Elementary School! She's tall and pretty and has long brown hair. And she loves holidays. Today she was wearing earrings that looked like colorful Easter eggs.

I dipped my brush into a jar of pink paint on my desk and colored in my bunny's nose. Then I swirled the brush into a jar of black paint and gave him a few cute whiskers.

Cassie leaned close to me. "Uh-oh," she

whispered. "Look who's coming over here."

Max Wade was heading toward my desk. He's a skinny kid with messy blond hair— and he's a little clumsy. Well, maybe more than a little. I glanced at his feet. Max's shoelaces were untied . . . as usual.

"Hey, Max," I called. "Your shoes are untied. Better fix them before you—"

Max tripped. "Whoa!"

He stumbled into my desk.

The jars of paint I was using wobbled. I caught the black one, but the pink one tipped over and splashed onto my mask.

"My bunny!" I cried.

"Sorry, Michelle," Max said, his face turning red. "I didn't mean it. I just came over to borrow your blue marker."

"Here." I handed it to him, and he went back to his desk in the first row.

Max never means it, I thought. But I wish he would be more careful! I stared at the big pink splotch on my mask and tried to figure out how to fix it.

"Use this, Michelle," Cassie said. She gave me a paper towel. "Maybe you can wipe it off."

I tried rubbing at the spot, but I just smeared the paint around. I sighed. "It's not working."

Mandy looked at my mask. "I've got an idea!" She dipped her paintbrush into the pink splotch—and swirled it into a circle. Then she made a circle on the other side of the mask. She had turned the ugly spots into two rosy cheeks. My bunny was better than ever!

"Awesome!" I said. "Thanks, Mandy!" I felt a lot better. I painted some more whiskers on my bunny mask. Then I suddenly remembered something. "Hey!" I exclaimed. "Spring vacation is almost here!"

Cassie and Mandy looked at me as if I were nuts.

"We know that, Michelle," Cassie said. "That's what we've been talking about all day!"

"Yeah, but I didn't write my column for the *Buzz* yet," I said. "I have to see if I got any letters."

The *Third-Grade Buzz* is our classroom newspaper. Everybody in our class helps write it. My job is to write the "Dear Michelle" advice column. Kids send me letters with questions, and I answer them. Each month I pick one letter to go into the *Buzz*.

It's a lot of work—and a lot of fun too!

But I wouldn't be able to give out any advice if I didn't look in my letter box. I raised my hand and asked Mrs. Ramirez if I could go check it. Mrs. R. nodded, and I was out the door in a flash.

The letter box sits on the floor right outside our classroom. It is decorated with glitter and paper hearts and the words *Dear Michelle* cut out from purple construction paper.

I carried the box back to my seat. Then I turned it over and gave it a shake. One letter with a pretty flowered border floated onto my desk. I couldn't wait to read it.

Julia "Bossy" Rossi turned around in her seat in front of me. She looked at the single letter and squinted at me. "If *I* wrote the advice column for the *Buzz*, I'd get lots of letters—not just one," she said.

"Too bad you don't," I said and squinted back. Julia was just mad because she wanted to write the advice column for the *Buzz*. But Mrs. Ramirez picked me fair and square!

Julia turned around in a huff and kicked her backpack into the aisle.

Then Mandy tapped me on the shoulder. "Better hide your bunny mask," she said. "Max is coming back."

Mandy was right. Max was heading my way. He had my marker in one hand and a tray of open paints in the other.

I looked at his feet and gulped. Max didn't notice that his shoelaces were untied again. He didn't notice Julia's backpack in the aisle either.

"Max . . ." I tried to warn him—too late.

"W-W-Whoa!" He fell over the backpack, and the tray of paints flew out of his hand!

"Oh, no!" I cried. "Paint shower! Everybody duck!"

Chapter Two

Pink, purple, yellow, and green paint rained down on the class. I tried to duck under my desk, but I felt wet drops splash onto my hair.

Then I heard Julia scream. Her pink dress was covered with bright green paint. She had green speckles of paint in her hair too.

"Julia looks like an alien from Mars!" Jeff Farrington said from his seat behind me. He started to laugh.

"No! She looks like an Easter egg!" Manuel Martinez joked.

Soon the entire class was cracking up and yelling.

"Quiet, class!" Mrs. Ramirez called out. "We need to clean up. Please line up for the bathroom. Everyone will go two at a time to get washed."

I got in line behind Cassie and Mandy. They had purple paint in their hair.

I reached up and touched my own strawberry-blond hair. I felt a sticky spot where the paint had landed. I looked at my fingers. Purple! "Hey, we match!" I told my friends. "Cool!"

"Yeah!" Mandy said. "Way to go, Max!"

Max was helping Mrs. Ramirez clean paint off the floor. His face was red again.

"Don't worry," Mrs. Ramirez was telling him. "Accidents happen."

"Well, I think we should all stay away from Max," Julia told everyone in line. She was standing behind me. "He's a walking disaster. And look at my dress. It's ruined!"

"But Max didn't do it on purpose," I said. "And anyway, your dress looks better now."

Cassie and Mandy giggled.

Julia stomped her foot. "I don't care. I hope Mrs. R. calls his parents. I hope she makes him stay after school and that he gets into lots and lots of trouble!"

I didn't want Max to get into trouble, but I *was* kind of glad that he didn't sit near me in class. If he did, I'd probably come home with a different stain on my clothes every day!

Everyone took turns washing up. Before we knew it, it was time to go home. Mandy, Cassie, and I raced to the school bus. When we were settled in our seats, I took out my "Dear Michelle" letter. With all the excitement in class, I hadn't had a chance to read it!

"Is that your letter for the *Buzz*?" Cassie said as the bus started up.

"What does it say?" Mandy asked.

I unfolded the paper and read the letter out loud:

Dear Michelle,

I want a pet more than anything! But my dad says I'm not responsible enough to take care of one. I would love to get a cute bunny for Easter. But how can I show my dad that I'm responsible with pets if I don't have a pet to show him with?

Signed,
Funny for Bunnies

"I love pets," Mandy said. "It's so cool when I get to take Swifty home over the weekend!" Swifty is the class's pet gerbil.

"Yeah, but taking care of a pet *is* hard work," I added. "I have to feed, walk, and play with my dog, Comet, every single day."

"But how can Funny for Bunnies prove he is responsible if he doesn't have a pet?" Cassie asked. "This is such a tough one, Michelle."

"I know," I said. "But I'll think of something. Maybe I'll even ask my family for help."

Between the nine of us we'd have to come up with at least one idea for Funny for Bunnies!

There's my dad, Danny, and my two older sisters, D.J. and Stephanie. My mom died when I was little, so Joey Gladstone moved in to help take care of us. He's my dad's best friend from college. But that's not all. Uncle Jesse moved in too. And he got married to Aunt Becky. Then they had twin boys, Nicky and Alex.

That's a lot of brainpower! I thought.

The bus stopped in front of my house. I

said good-bye to my friends and got off. Then I reached into my backpack and pulled out my bunny mask. I slipped it onto my face and hopped into the house.

Uncle Joey was by the coat closet, putting on his jacket. "Hi, bunny," he said. "Do you know where Michelle is?"

I shook my head and giggled. "Nope!"

"Well, then, do you know how Easter Bunnies stay in shape?" he asked.

"How?" I asked through the mask.

"They *eggs-ercise*!" Uncle Joey cried. "Get it? Get it?"

I laughed and laughed. Uncle Joey is so funny! He loves to tell jokes. In fact, he loves it so much that it's his job. He's a comedian.

I pulled off my mask and said, "Surprise!"

"Hey, it's not a bunny. It's Michelle!" Uncle Joey cried.

"Are you going out somewhere?" I asked.

13

"Just to get the mail," he said.

"I'll do it!" I said. Maybe I'd find a letter in the mailbox for me!

"Thanks," Uncle Joey said. "Now hop to it!"

"Okay!" I hopped over to the mailbox by the curb, bunny-style. Then I opened it and peeked inside. Wow! There were lots of letters. I looked through them as I walked back to the house. Nothing for me. Darn!

But then something caught my eye. It was a bright pink piece of paper—an ad for something.

A huge grin spread across my face as I read it. It was the answer to my problem. Now I knew exactly what to tell Funny for Bunnies!

Chapter Three

"It's almost time to eat, Michelle," Dad called to me a little while later. "Would you please set the table?"

"Be right down!" I yelled to him from my room. Stephanie and I shared it. I was doing my homework at my desk. But I hadn't written my letter to Funny for Bunnies yet. I wanted to ask my dad a question first.

Stephanie was lying on her bed across the room, petting our golden retriever, Comet, and reading a magazine. "Mmm. I wonder what Dad made for dinner," she said. "It sure smells good!"

"I don't know, but I'm hungry!" I said. My stomach rumbled. I ran down the stairs and into the kitchen. "What's for dinner, Dad?"

Dad stood in front of the oven. He wore an apron and had an oven mitt on each hand. He carefully reached inside the oven and pulled out a sizzling pan. "Homemade pizza!" he said proudly. "I'm trying out a new recipe for the show." My dad is not only a great cook, he's the host of a TV show. It's called *Good Morning, San Francisco!*

"I love pizza!" I cried, and I hurried to set the table.

Once the table was ready, Dad called everyone to dinner. Uncle Jesse came in carrying Nicky, and Aunt Becky walked in holding Alex. They put the twins into their high chairs and sat down.

"My nose led me right here," Stephanie said. She sat next to me.

Uncle Joey and D.J. were the last to arrive. Finally Dad began cutting the pizza and dishing it out for us.

I chowed down on a cheesy slice, and I couldn't stop smiling. I was eating my favorite food, and I had a great idea to give to Funny for Bunnies.

What could be better?

"I'm glad to see you like the pizza, Michelle," Dad said to me. "But you haven't stopped grinning since you sat down."

"It's the best, Dad," I told him. "But that's not the only reason I'm so happy. You see, I—"

"I know why!" D.J. interrupted. "You can't wait for spring break. Right, Michelle? No homework, no school . . ."

"Yeah, but—" I started.

"And Easter!" Stephanie piped in. "Don't forget about that!"

"That's true," Aunt Becky said. "And

who's coming to visit on Easter?" she asked Nicky and Alex.

"The Easter Bunny!" the twins cried at the same time.

"That bunny had better not forget me this year," Uncle Jesse said, frowning. "Last Easter I didn't get a basket!"

Aunt Becky laughed. "Don't worry, honey," she said. "If he forgets you again, I'm sure the boys will share their chocolate bunnies with you."

"I *am* excited about the break and Easter," I said quickly. "But I'm also happy about something *else*." Boy, I thought, sometimes it's tough to get a word in around my house!

"What, sweetie?" Dad asked.

That's when I told them about the letter from Funny for Bunnies—and how Funny for Bunnies needed to be responsible before he could get a pet.

"That *is* a tricky one," Uncle Jesse said.

"But I totally lucked out!" I said. "There was a flier in the mail today from Old MacDonald's Petting Zoo. I've got it right here." I reached into my jeans pocket and pulled out the pink paper. It was crumpled from being in my pocket, so I tried to flatten it out.

"The zoo is looking for kids to help with their big Easter party," I went on. "They run a camp for two days. You get to learn how to take care of bunnies, and you help get the zoo ready for the party. It sounds like a lot of fun!"

"Let me take a look at that," Dad said.

I handed him the flier. "See? If Funny for Bunnies helps out at the zoo and learns how to take care of bunnies . . ."

"Then maybe Funny will get a bunny?" Dad asked with a grin.

"You got it!" I looked around at everyone.

"Do you think that's good advice?" I asked.

"I don't know, Michelle." Stephanie shook her head. Her long blond hair swung around her shoulders. Her eyes opened wide. "Small animals can be *very* dangerous. Sure, they look all cute and fluffy, but you never know. A girl in my class almost got her finger bitten off by an angry guinea pig!"

I gasped. "Really?"

"Uh-huh." Stephanie wiggled her pinky and started making chomping noises.

"Don't listen to her," D.J. said. "She's just teasing you."

"Well, I think it's great advice," Aunt Becky told me.

"Me too," Dad agreed. "Would you please pass the salad? All this talk about bunnies makes me want to eat some lettuce!"

"Well, there's one more thing," I said. "The camp sounds awesome . . . and I love bunnies . . . and I've been doing really well in school. . . . Do you think *I* could go to bunny camp too?" I smiled my sweetest smile at Dad. "Can I? Please?"

Dad glanced at the flier. "It's the first two days of your vacation. Are you sure that's what you want to do?"

I thought about it. I wouldn't be able to sleep late or watch cartoons in my pajamas on those days. But I would have the rest of the week off. And hanging out with bunnies sounded like so much fun!

"Yes, I'm sure!" I said.

Dad smiled. "Okay, Michelle. Bunny camp, it is!"

"Cool!" I shoved the last few bites of my pizza into my mouth as fast as I could. "May I be excused?" I asked. "I have a letter to write."

"Sure," Dad said.

I wiped my mouth with a napkin and

ran upstairs to write my column for the *Third-Grade Buzz*.

Dear Funny for Bunnies,

Having a pet is fun, but it does take a lot of hard work. I should know. I have a dog named Comet. I have to walk and feed him every day. Your dad might not be sure if you can do all these things.

So prove it to him! Old MacDonald's Petting Zoo is letting kids help out during spring vacation. They'll teach you how to take care of bunnies. And you get to decorate the place for an Easter party. Help out at the zoo, and learn how to take care of bunnies. Then your dad will have to let you get a pet! It sounds like so much fun that I'm going to go. I hope I'll see you there!

And that's my advice! Good luck!

Love,
Michelle

I tucked the letter into my backpack. I knew my answer would be printed in the newspaper later that week. I just didn't know if Funny for Bunnies would take my advice!

Chapter Four

The very next Monday Dad dropped me off at Old MacDonald's Petting Zoo. I couldn't wait to play with the bunnies, dye Easter eggs, and make decorations for the zoo's Easter party. Camp was going to be so cool!

I stood with a group of bunny campers near the front gate. I looked around at the other kids and wondered if Funny for Bunnies had taken my advice.

I spotted Gracie Chin and Manuel Martinez from my class. They waved to me, and I waved back.

Was one of them Funny for Bunnies?

I was about to go over there, when a voice stopped me.

"I knew you would be here, Michelle," a girl said.

I whirled around and saw Julia Rossi. She was sitting on a low brick wall that had farm animals painted on it.

Julia hopped off the wall and walked over to me. "I read about this bunny camp in your column. I thought for once you might be giving out good advice. So I decided to come."

No way! Julia *never* said anything nice about my column. Never, *ever*! Did this mean that Julia "Bossy" Rossi was Funny for Bunnies?

I felt bad for the bunny that had to go home with *her*! But I decided to be nice.

"Camp is going to be great!" I said. Then I spotted Max Wade coming toward the group. He was holding a box of chocolate milk and a doughnut.

Julia saw him too and groaned. "Oh, no, not *him*. The bunnies should run for their lives!" she said.

"Max isn't *that* bad," I said, looking over at him. He bit into his doughnut. Then he took a drink of chocolate milk, and the whole thing spilled down the front of his shirt!

Oh boy, I thought. Maybe the bunnies *should* be worried. Or better yet, maybe the owners of the zoo should be worried. I hope they have a lot of cleaning supplies!

Just then a woman with a long red braid asked everyone to come inside the petting zoo. Standing next to her was a young man with dark brown hair.

The kids entered the zoo and gathered around them.

"Hi, my name is Lauren," the woman

said. "And this is Gary." She pointed to the man. "I'll be teaching you how to take care of the bunnies. And Gary will be helping us. We've got lots of fun things to do. Let's walk over to where the bunnies are kept. On the way there you can see some of the other animals we have."

Lauren led the campers down a brick path and past a big red barn. There were about twelve kids altogether.

Lauren showed us some sheep and goats—and some ponies too. We stopped by a low pen and watched a bunch of chickens clucking around. Then Lauren pointed out the zoo's garden, which grew beautiful flowers and vegetables.

"What's that smell?" Julia wrinkled her nose as we continued down the path.

I sniffed the air. Yuck! Something did stink. Then I saw what it was. We were passing a pigpen. Inside, chubby pigs with white and black spots were sleeping in the sun. Sticky mud oozed out from underneath the fence.

Max came running over. He jumped into line next to me—and landed in a mud puddle. Mud splattered all over my sparkly purple sneakers. My favorite sneakers!

"Oops! Sorry, Michelle," Max said.

I looked at my dirty shoes. It's a good thing Dad is a neat freak, I thought. He'll know how to get these clean.

"It's okay," I told Max.

"And this is the learning center," Lauren said, stopping in front of a white building. "We have lots of different kinds of animals in here. But we're going to call it the bunny building. Easter is coming, and the bunnies are very special this week." She looked over the group. "So, will you help me get ready for the coolest Easter party ever?"

Everyone clapped and cheered.

Lauren and Gary led us inside the bunny building and to a yellow room that was bright and cheerful. Tables and chairs were set up at the back of the room. A big metal pen was in the center. And the bunnies were inside it!

They looked so cute, hopping around and munching on hay. I couldn't wait to play with them!

"Okay!" Lauren said. "We've got lots to do. We have to dye eggs for the Easter egg hunt and make party favors. . . ."

"And, of course, take care of the bunnies," Gary added. "And on the day of the party we'll announce which one of these guys will be the zoo's official Easter Bunny!"

"So who wants to learn about bunnies?" Lauren asked.

We all shouted, "Meeeeee!"

"Good! Everyone find a buddy," Lauren said, "and we'll get started."

The kids raced around, trying to pick out partners.

Gracie was on the other side of the room. I ran over to ask her if she wanted to be my buddy.

"Sorry, Michelle," she said. "Manuel already asked me."

"Oh, okay. See you later!" I didn't have time to talk. I needed to find a partner—fast. And I didn't want it to be Julia! But who else was there?

Someone crashed into me from behind.

"Oof!" I tumbled to the floor. "Hey, what's the big idea?" I said. When I looked up, I saw Max standing over me. I wasn't surprised.

"Sorry, Michelle!" He helped me up. "I ran over here. I had to tell you something. I had to say thanks."

"No problem," I said. "But what are you thanking me for?"

He looked around to see if anybody was listening. Then he lowered his voice to a whisper. "For the great idea," he said. "I'm Funny for Bunnies. Want to be my partner?"

Chapter Five

I gulped. Clumsy Max is Funny for Bunnies? And he wants to be my partner? Oh, no!

I looked at Max. He smiled at me.

"So, Michelle," Max said. "What do you say?"

"Ummmm . . ." I glanced around the room. There were only a few kids left without buddies—including Julia. Max *had* to be better than her . . . right? "Okay," I said.

"Cool!" Max cried. "High five!" He held up his right hand and grinned at me.

I slapped it hard and smiled back.

Max was really nice. Maybe this wouldn't be so bad!

Lauren clapped her hands to get the group's attention. She and Gary were standing in front of the bunny pen. "Okay, kids! It's time to meet the bunnies!" she said.

Max yelled, "All right!"

"Awesome!" another kid cried.

"I'm going first," Julia said.

"But we have to keep calm and speak quietly while we play with them," Gary said. "I don't want you to pick up the bunnies just yet, but you can pet them. They love that!"

"And one more thing," Lauren added. "The door to this room must be kept closed at all times. If the bunnies get out of here, they could get hurt!"

Lauren had us all sit with our buddies

at the tables near the back of the room. Then she sent a few kids at a time to the bunny pen.

"Gracie and Manuel, Jared and Michael, come on up and meet the bunnies!" Lauren said.

"I bet you didn't know I was Funny for Bunnies, did you, Michelle?" Max asked as we waited for our turn. "My dad thought the camp was a great idea," he said. "If I do a good job here, he says I can get a bunny! And I'm going to call it Snuggles. That's a cool name for a bunny, right, Michelle?"

"Sounds good to me." I had to smile. Max was so excited!

Lauren called out the next two groups. "Michelle and Max, Julia and Danielle, it's your turn to visit the bunnies. Come on up here."

Max and I raced to the bunny pen.

There were white bunnies, brown bunnies, and gray bunnies. And some had different colored spots.

I reached in to stroke a fluffy gray one with long floppy ears. He was very soft! Then a white-and-black bunny with ears that stood straight up sniffed my hand. How cute! I wanted to pet them all!

Julia was at the pen with her buddy— a girl I didn't know.

"You're lucky you've got me for a partner, Danielle," Julia was saying. "I know lots about bunnies."

I saw Danielle roll her eyes, and I giggled. It looked as if Danielle thought Julia was pretty bossy too!

Julia pointed to a big puffy white bunny in the pen. "This bunny is something special. I'm going to call him Mr. Fluffy. I'll bet he's going to be the zoo's official Easter Bunny!"

I went over to see what Julia was talking about. Mr. Fluffy was pretty. But was he the best bunny of all?

I looked around the pen. A tiny brown bunny caught my eye. She was sitting all alone in a corner.

"I like that bunny, Max." I pointed to the tiny brown one. "I'm going to call her Pixie."

Max was petting a little gray bunny. "She's pretty cute," he said and waved to her. "Hi, Pixie!"

Pixie sat in the corner. She looked at Max and twitched her nose.

"I think *Pixie* will be the zoo's Easter Bunny!" I said.

"No way," Julia said. "With Mr. Fluffy around, Pixie doesn't have a chance!"

"Oh, yeah?" Max stood up straight. "Pixie is a lot cuter than Mr. Fluffy! Pixie is going to be the Easter Bunny!"

Mr. Fluffy hopped close to Julia. She patted him on the head.

I tried to call Pixie, but she stayed in the corner.

"That rabbit is too shy to be an Easter Bunny," Julia said. "I know about these things."

"Pixie isn't too shy!" I told her. "Maybe she's just tired."

I wish Julia would get tired of thinking she knows everything, I thought.

Julia started to walk away. "Whatever you say, Michelle," she said. "Let's go, Danielle. We're done here."

Danielle followed Julia back to their table.

"Come on, Pixie." I put my hand in the pen. I snapped my fingers. "Come here, girl!"

Pixie didn't budge.

I didn't want to say it, but Julia might

be right. Maybe Pixie was too shy to be the zoo's official Easter Bunny.

"Hey, maybe we could teach Pixie a trick," Max said. "It would make her an extra special bunny. Maybe then she wouldn't be so shy."

I was impressed. Max's idea was pretty good. "If Pixie knew a trick, then Lauren might even pick her to be the Easter Bunny," I said. "That would be so cool!"

"Time to dye Easter eggs!" Lauren said later, after we all had a turn to meet the bunnies.

"Yay!" I cheered from my table. Max was sitting next to me.

Gracie and Manuel bounced in their seats one table over.

Julia sat quietly at her table with her hands folded on top. She made her partner, Danielle, sit the same way.

"If you need supplies, ask me for help," Gary said. He disappeared into a big closet—and came out with six boxes of hard-boiled eggs. Then he brought out a bunch of trays that had cups and spoons on them. Each cup was filled with a different colored dye. He placed one tray and one box on each table.

Max and I looked over our cups of dye. "These are all red," I said to Max. "We need to ask Gary for some different colors. I want to make a pink egg and a blue one. Pink and blue are my favorite colors."

"I want purple," Max said. "I'll go ask Gary."

I might as well make a red egg while I'm waiting, I thought. I grabbed an egg and carefully dropped it into the dye. I waited a few minutes. Then I fished out the egg with my spoon and put it back in the box to dry.

Now I was ready to dye my pink egg. But where was Max?

I spotted him near the bunny pen. He was holding a tray of dyes in one hand.

"Hey, cute little bunnies," Max said. He reached into the pen to pet a bunny.

Uh-oh. That's not a good idea, I thought. I remembered what happened in Mrs. Ramirez's class last week—when he spilled the paint. Max could drop the dye into the bunny pen!

I stood up. "Hey, Max, be careful!" I called.

"Huh?" Max turned to me. The cups of dye slid off the tray—and into the pen! Yellow, pink, green, and purple dyes splattered all over the bunnies. "Oh, no!" he cried.

"Mr. Fluffy!" Julia screamed, and she ran to the bunny pen. Mr. Fluffy's white fur had green splotches all over it!

Lauren hurried to the pen too. So did the rest of the class.

I stared at the bunnies. Pink, purple, green, and yellow-spotted bunnies stared back at me.

Then I looked at Max. His face was bright red. His lips were quivering, and his eyes were filling with tears.

"It's okay, Max," Lauren said softly. "The dye won't hurt the bunnies. But we need to wash it off right now. Gary, I need your help!" she called out.

Gary walked over. "Oh boy," he said. "Looks like these bunnies are ready for Easter!"

Lauren pulled the bunnies out of the pen one by one and handed them to Gary. He brought them into another room to wash them off.

"It was just an accident," I whispered to Max. "It could have happened to anybody!"

41

"Oh, no, it couldn't," Julia said. "Only Mr. Spill-It-All could make such a mess. He should go home right now before he hurts the bunnies."

That was so mean! "Maybe *you're* the one who should go home," I told her.

"I'm not going anywhere, Michelle," she said. "And neither is Mr. Fluffy. So get used to it!" Then she turned and walked back to her seat.

"Maybe she's right, Michelle," Max said. "I'm no good at taking care of bunnies. My dad is never going to let me have one. Never!"

What could I say? Max wouldn't get a bunny if things kept going this way. But I didn't want him to give up!

"Forget about Julia. She doesn't know what she's talking about," I told him. "You'll show your dad that you deserve a bunny!"

Max sniffled. "You mean it?"

"You bet," I said. "You are going to get a bunny, Max. And I'll help you—no matter what it takes!"

"Really?" Max's face brightened. "Cool!" he said. "Because my dad will be here any minute!"

Chapter Six

"Are you joking?" I asked. How could I help Max if we had only a few minutes to practice?

"Nope. My dad is coming by this afternoon," Max said. "He wants to watch me with the bunnies—to see how I do."

"But why not wait until tomorrow?" I asked. "Today is only your first day!"

Max shrugged. "He said he wanted to come. But I've got you, partner! We'll show him that I'm good with bunnies, right?"

"Sure!" I said. But I wasn't *really* sure. I didn't know if my advice to Funny for

Bunnies would work. Not when Funny was Max!

Soon it was time for lunch. Lauren and Gary took us outside for a picnic in the zoo's garden. Afterward we went back to the bunny room to learn how to handle the bunnies.

I looked around nervously. Was Max's dad here yet?

A man I had never seen before sat on a chair in a corner. He waved and smiled at Max.

Max waved back. "That's my dad!" he whispered to me. "You're still going to help me, right?"

I nodded. It was time for some serious bunny business!

Lauren showed us the right way to pick up a bunny. "Stand behind the bunny. Put one hand under its backside. Put your other under its chest and lift. Be very gentle."

She took a few of the bunnies out of the pen so we could practice. We all took turns picking up the bunnies.

I went right to Pixie, and I did exactly as Lauren said. It worked! Pixie didn't seem nervous at all.

Neither did any of the other bunnies. Julia was holding Mr. Fluffy. Gracie had just put down a gray bunny. Then Manuel took a turn and held it. Some boys in the corner were practicing with a brown rabbit.

Now it was Max's turn to hold a bunny. He stood behind Pixie and started to lift her up—by the back of the neck!

"Uh, Max." I snuck a peek at Max's dad. Good thing he was busy talking to Lauren. He hadn't seen Max's mistake. "That's not how you pick up a bunny," I whispered. "Let me show you."

I stood behind Pixie and put one hand underneath her chest. Then I put my other hand under the back end. I slowly lifted her up. "See?" I said. "Now you try."

Max took a deep breath. He stood behind Pixie—and then lifted her up the right way!

"Awesome!" I said, glancing over at his dad again. Mr. Wade was watching us now—and smiling! That's a good sign, I thought.

A few minutes later Lauren and Gary began collecting the bunnies and putting them back into the pen.

"Good job!" Lauren said. "Now it's time to take care of the bunnies." She pointed at Max and me. "Would you guys help me feed them?" she asked.

"Yes!" I said, pumping a fist in the air. I hoped we would get that job.

"Gary will give you the food," Lauren said. "Put one scoop of bunny chow into each dish."

"Julia and Danielle," she continued. "You can empty out the litter boxes. Okay?"

Julia groaned—and Max and I started laughing. That was a stinky job!

Lauren gave bunny-care assignments to the rest of the kids. Then everyone got to work.

Max went into the closet to get the bunny food from Gary.

I emptied out the old food that was left in the bunnies' dishes.

"I've got the food, Michelle," Max said. He was carrying a huge bag of rabbit chow. It looked pretty heavy. Then I noticed something else. His shoes were untied—again!

I ran over to help Max carry the bag to the bunny pen. I didn't want him to trip and spill it all over the place.

"Thanks, Michelle," he said.

"No problem," I said. Then I pointed at

his laces. "Maybe you should tie those tighter so you don't fall."

"Good idea." Max double-knotted his shoelaces. Then he lifted the bunny chow by himself. He started to pour the bag of food into a little dish.

"Wait!" I said, stopping him. "You can't pour that big bag of food into a tiny dish. The stuff will spill everywhere."

Max glanced at his dad, then back at me. "I forgot how Lauren said we should do it," he said.

I reached into the bag and pulled out the silver scoop. I handed it to Max. "Lauren said we should use this. One scoop of food in each dish."

"Oh. Okay." Max scooped out some bunny chow and poured it into Pixie's bowl.

Lauren stopped by with Mr. Wade to see how we were getting along. "Nice job, Max," she said.

"You really seem to know what you're doing," Mr. Wade told Max.

"Thanks, Dad!" Max smiled.

That's another good sign. Maybe Max *will* get his bunny, I thought happily.

After we finished feeding the bunnies, Max carried the bag of food out of the pen and left the gate open behind him.

I remembered that Lauren said it was important to keep the gate closed so that the bunnies wouldn't get out. I dashed to the gate and shut it tightly.

"Good work, everyone," Lauren said. "Now let's make some party favors for tomorrow!"

We raced to our seats at the back of the room. Gary passed out some colorful plastic eggshells that could be separated in two. Lauren handed out bags of colorful jelly beans.

Max and I popped open our plastic eggs

and filled them with the candy. The eggs we had dyed earlier were drying in a box on our table.

"These Easter eggs look so cool," Max said. "I'm going to show them to Lauren and my dad."

Lauren and Mr. Wade were talking by the windows on the other side of the room.

Max checked his shoelaces to make sure they were still tied. "I don't want to trip," he said with a grin. Then he grabbed our box of eggs and started over there.

Max waved to the bunnies as he passed their pen. He didn't see the bag of bunny litter in his path. He was going to fall right over it—and break our eggs right in front of his dad!

I raced over there and pushed the bag out of the way.

Max walked right past me. He handed the tray to Lauren. "These Easter eggs are all dried. Don't they look nice?" he asked.

"Yes, they do, Max," Lauren said. "You're doing an excellent job today."

Max grinned. "Thanks!"

It was almost time to go home, and the class helped Lauren and Gary clean up the art supplies.

Max picked up the tray of dyes we had used, then stopped. "Uh, Michelle?" he said. "I haven't had too much luck with this stuff so far. Maybe you should put it away."

I laughed. "Good idea," I said, and I put it in the supply closet.

We both finished cleaning, and Mr. Wade came over to our table.

"Max, I'm very impressed," he said. "If you do this well tomorrow, you'll get a bunny for sure!"

"Wow, Dad!" Max said. "Excellent! Did you hear that, Michelle?"

"That's so cool!" I said. I gave Max my biggest smile. But then I frowned. I just remembered something. Something awful!

Max and I had bragged to Julia that little Pixie—not Mr. Fluffy—was going to be the zoo's official Easter Bunny. But we didn't have time to teach Pixie how to do a special trick by tomorrow.

Would our shy bunny stand a chance?

Chapter Seven

"See you later, Dad!" I yelled when he dropped me off at bunny camp the next morning.

Dad waved and drove away in his mini-van. I had asked him take me to the petting zoo a little early today.

That's because I had a plan!

I liked Max's idea of teaching Pixie a trick. If Pixie learned a trick, she'd be picked as the zoo's Easter Bunny for sure!

But first I had to teach her the trick. And I didn't have much time. The Easter party was in just a few hours.

I raced down the brick path all the way to the bunny building. Maybe Lauren will let me have some time alone with Pixie, I thought. Once Max shows up, I'll be too busy helping him get a bunny. I won't have time to teach Pixie anything.

I opened the door to the bunny room, hoping to find Lauren. She wasn't there. *Max* was.

"What are you doing here so early?" I asked him.

"I came to wash out the bunny pens," Max said. "You helped me so much yesterday, Michelle. I wanted to prove I could do something good for the bunnies all by myself!"

"Wash out the bunny pens?" I wasn't so sure he should be doing that. "Did you ask Lauren if you could?"

Max shook his head. "I couldn't find her. Besides, I want it to be a surprise."

Hmm . . . How can I ask Lauren if I can train Pixie if she's not around? Oh, well, I thought. I bet she won't mind. Besides, I'll be extra careful. And Pixie's trick will be a surprise too!

"I think I'm going to teach Pixie a trick," I told Max. "Let me know if you need any help."

"Don't worry, I won't," Max said. He went to get cleaning supplies from the closet.

I found Pixie and took her out of the bunny pen—just the way Lauren had shown us. "Could you get me some bunny treats?" I called to Max.

"What for?" Max asked.

"When we teach Comet a new trick, we always use treats," I said. "I'm going to try it with Pixie."

Max went back into the closet for the treats and gave them to me. Then he began taking the other bunnies out of the pen.

"I made sure the door to the bunny room is closed," he said. "The bunnies will be fine. I'm going to do this right!"

I took Pixie into a corner of the room. I held up a stick a few inches off the floor. I was going to teach Pixie how to jump over the stick!

"Come on, Pixie," I said. "Jump over the stick!"

Pixie stared at me. She wiggled her nose.

"You can do it!" I said. I patted the floor on the other side of the stick. "Jump!"

Pixie turned away from the stick.

I looked at the clock on the wall. "Please, Pixie," I said. "We don't have much time!" I turned her around and held out the stick again. "Just try it."

Then I heard a loud crash!

"Oh, no!" Max cried.

I looked up. Bubbles were flooding out of the sides of the bunny pen. The floor around it was wet and slippery.

"What happened?" I asked.

"I put some soap in a bucket. Then I filled it with water. I must have used too much soap," Max said. "And then I knocked over the bucket!"

"We've got to clean up this mess before anybody finds out," I told him. "Especially your dad! I'll get a mop."

I ran out of the bunny room and into the hallway. I had seen Lauren go into a broom closet yesterday. Maybe there was a mop inside.

I found the closet and yanked open the door.

Aha! A mop was leaning against a stack of shelves! I grabbed it and hurried back to the bunny room.

Max was bent over the bunny pen, trying

to scoop up bubbles with a paper towel.

It wasn't working.

I handed Max the mop. "Here. Use this," I said.

Then I stopped. I got a weird butterfly feeling in my stomach as I looked around the room. Something wasn't right.

There was Max . . . the mop . . . the bunny pen . . . the bubbles . . .

I gasped. "But where are all the bunnies?"

Chapter Eight

"The bunnies were all right here in the room," Max said. "I closed the door so they wouldn't get out!"

But now the door to the bunny room was wide open!

"Oh, no!" I smacked my forehead. "I forgot to close the door when I went to get the mop!"

"Don't panic," Max said. "Maybe the bunnies are around here somewhere."

We looked under the tables. We looked under the chairs. But we didn't see a single rabbit.

"We've got to get those bunnies back—fast!" I said.

"Shouldn't we find Lauren and tell her?" Max asked.

"There's no time!" I ran out of the bunny building—and almost stepped on a gray floppy-eared rabbit! It was sitting right by the door, chewing on some grass. I scooped it up and carried it back to the bunny room.

"Wait, Michelle!" Max mopped out the pen, and then I put the bunny inside it.

"Oh boy, oh boy, oh boy," I muttered. This was a disaster!

"I never should have taken the bunnies out of their pen," Max said. "This is all my fault."

"No, it's *my* fault," I said. "I'm the one who left the door to the room open!"

But we couldn't worry about all that now. We had to find the bunnies! We ran down the zoo pathway. Max tripped over a rock and knocked into me.

"Ow!" I went flying onto the grass. When I looked up, I saw two white rabbits lying in the sun.

Max started to apologize, but I cut him off. "Forget it, Max." I pointed at the bunnies. "Just grab them."

We took the bunnies and raced to put them back in the pen. Then we went outside again.

We zoomed past the chicken pen. Out of the corner of my eye I noticed something strange. One of the chicks was brown with white spots. And it had long, floppy ears. It was a bunny!

"Look!" I called to Max.

He saw the bunny and grabbed it. We raced back to the bunny building, and Max set the bunny down in the pen.

"What about inside the building?" he

said. "We didn't look in the rooms where other animals are kept."

"Good thinking, Max," I said. "Let's go!" We hurried down the hallway and ran into the first room we found open.

"Whoa!" Max said. Small glass tanks were set up on tables around the room. Inside the tanks were turtles, lizards, and snakes!

"This must be the reptile room," I said.

A huge tank rested on the floor. Next to the tank sat a bunny, licking its front paws. Inside the tank a green snake was rising onto its tail. Its narrow eyes were focused on the bunny. The snake's skinny tongue flicked out. It looked hungry!

"Ahhh!" My heart pounded in my chest. I grabbed the bunny. "Let's get out of here!"

We raced back into the hall. A black-and-white rabbit hopped in front of us.

Max picked it up. Then we put both bunnies into the pen.

We tried all the other open rooms, but we didn't find another bunny.

"The rest of them have to be outside," I said.

We dashed over to the barn where the sheep and goats were kept—and we found a fluffy bunny sitting on a pile of hay.

"Got him!" I said. Then I heard a terrible squeal!

"I think it's coming from the pigpen!" Max cried, and we hurried over there.

Sure enough, sitting right next to the pigpen was Mr. Fluffy. A terrified piglet squealed in alarm at the bunny.

Max scooped up Mr. Fluffy, and we put the two rabbits back into their pen.

Then we counted the bunnies.

"Two bunnies are still missing," I said. "And one of them is Pixie!"

"I know where we can look," Max said. "The garden!"

We sprinted over to the zoo's garden. A black bunny sat in a vegetable patch, munching on some lettuce.

"That's a smart bunny!" I said. I picked up the bunny and took it back to the pen.

Now we had to find Pixie.

We searched everywhere. Back in the bunny room. In the bathroom. Max even looked under a rock!

But Pixie wasn't in any of those places— and we couldn't come up with one more place to look for her.

Oh, no, I thought. What if Pixie is lost . . . forever?

Chapter Nine

Max and I sat on the steps of the bunny building. I buried my head in my hands. The sun shone in the bright blue sky. It was a perfect spring day. But Max and I felt awful!

Where could Pixie be?

Suddenly music began playing in the distance. I lifted my head. The party! I had forgotten all about it. Lauren had told us the Easter egg hunt was going to be held on the front lawn of the zoo.

I bet Lauren had been setting up for the party while we were looking for the bunnies. And now the party was going to start without us!

I stood up and held out my hand. "We won't find Pixie by sitting around and feeling sorry for ourselves!" I said, and I helped Max up.

"Okay, partner," he said. "Let's find that bunny!"

Max wandered off to look through a bunch of red and yellow tulips blooming nearby. "Wow!" he shouted.

"Pixie?" I raced over. "Did you find her?"

"No," Max said. "But look." He picked up a small green frog sitting next to a red tulip. "He's so cool!"

"You're right," I said, staring at the frog. "But we still have to find Pixie!"

Think, brain, think! I told myself. Where is the one place we haven't looked?

"I've got it!" I snapped my fingers. "The

supply closet in the bunny room. We forgot to look in there!"

"Let's check it out," Max said. He gently put the frog into his jacket pocket and followed me back to the bunny room. When we got there, I rushed into the big closet.

Large metal shelves held supplies for the small animals. Big bags of bunny chow and hay sat on the floor. One of the bags was open.

And there, munching on a strand of hay . . . was Pixie!

Pixie looked at us and wiggled her nose.

"There you are!" I said to Pixie. "You had me really worried." I called to Max, "I found her!"

Max came running into the closet. He tripped over a bag of bunny chow and knocked into the closet door. "Is Pixie okay?" he asked.

The door began to swing closed.

"Max, watch out!" I cried.

Too late! The door shut with a slam.

Max grabbed the doorknob and tried to turn it. But it wouldn't budge!

"Uh-oh," Max said. "We're locked in!"

Chapter Ten

I banged my fists on the door. "Help us!" I cried. "We're locked in the closet. Lauren! Gary! Anybody!"

I pounded some more, but nobody answered.

I sighed and looked around the closet. It was dark, and I couldn't see any windows. I felt around on the wall until I came to a switch. I flicked it on, and light filled the closet.

Max sat on the closet floor. He was holding Pixie in his lap and gently petting the bunny.

"I'm trying to keep Pixie calm," Max said. "She got a little upset with all the banging and yelling."

"Oops! I forgot that bunnies don't like loud noises." I smiled. "Hey, you're holding Pixie like a pro! I guess you've got the hang of it."

"Uh-huh," Max said with a smile.

I looked around the closet again. I wondered if there was another way out. Then I saw something move on one of the shelves!

I gasped. "What's that?"

I took a closer look and realized it was the frog Max had found. It was in a clear glass tank.

It looked at me and said, "Ribbit!"

"Ribbit to you too," I said.

"I still had him in my pocket," Max said. "I didn't want to squish him. There was an empty tank on the shelf, so I put him inside it."

Wow. Max was doing a great job with Pixie—*and* the frog. "If only your Dad could see you now!" I told him.

"If only *anybody* could see us now," Max said. "Then we could get out of here!"

I searched the closet. There was no way out except the door. We would just have to wait until someone came and unlocked it.

"At least we have food to eat," I joked. "Lots of hay, bunny chow, and treats!"

Max laughed. "We'll turn into bunnies if we eat all that!"

"Bunny treats!" I cried. I just had a great idea. "We don't have to waste time while we're stuck in here. We can practice the trick with Pixie!"

"Great idea!" Max said. "I'll get the treats!"

"And we can use this." I grabbed a nearby broomstick. "Pixie can jump over it!"

We set up a little bunny hurdle in a

corner of the closet. I found some bricks and made two low stacks. Then I rested the broomstick on the bricks.

Now all we had to do was get Pixie to jump!

"Come on, Pixie!" Max said. "Do it like this!" He jumped over the broomstick.

Pixie twitched her nose.

"You can do it, Pixie!" I said. I held a bunny treat on the other side of the broom. "Jump if you want it!"

Pixie wiggled her tail. She smelled the treat. Then she began hopping around.

"Mmm. I bet this treat tastes good," I said. "Come and get it!"

Pixie ran underneath the broomstick. She gobbled the treat from my hand.

"Hey! No fair!" I laughed.

Max took away one brick from each stack to make the hurdle lower. "Now she can't run under it," he said.

Pixie twitched her nose again. She sniffed my hand. She was looking for another treat!

"If you want another one, you're going to have to jump for it!" I told the bunny. I patted her on the head. Then I held the treat on the other side of the stick.

"Jump for the treat, Pixie!" Max called.

Pixie sniffed the air again. Then she did another nose twitch. And *then* she jumped over the stick!

"All right!" I cried and fed Pixie the treat.

"She did it," Max said. He gave me a high five!

I knelt down beside Pixie. She jumped into my lap, and I petted her softly. "I knew you could do it," I told her.

"I just wish we could show Pixie's trick to Lauren," Max admitted. "But we're stuck in here!"

I shook my head. "If we don't get out soon, we'll miss the entire party."

Max frowned. "And the Easter egg hunt too."

"Shh!" I put a finger to my lips. "I think I hear something." I ran to the closet door. It sounded like voices—people were calling our names!

"Michelle! Max!" I heard Lauren shout. "Where are you?"

"Lauren is looking for us!" I said to Max. Then I banged on the door. "We're in here!" I cried.

Max came over and started pounding on the door too.

"They have to hear us," I said to Max. "They just have to!"

Chapter Eleven

The door to the supply closet swung open. In walked my dad!

"Dad!" I yelled. I ran to give him a huge hug. "I'm so glad to see you!"

"Whoa!" Dad said. He squeezed me tightly. "I'm glad to see you too. We came to the zoo for the party. But Lauren said she never saw you this morning. I was so worried!"

Lauren walked into the closet along with Max's mom and dad.

"We've been looking for you everywhere," Lauren said.

"What happened?" Mr. Wade asked. "And how did you end up locked in the closet?"

Max and I glanced at each other.

"It's kind of a long story," I explained. "Max and I both came to camp early today. I wanted to teach Pixie a trick. And Max wanted to do something nice for Lauren."

"I started cleaning the bunny pens. But I put too much soap in. And then I spilled the big bucket of water," Max said.

"I ran to get a mop, but I left the door to the bunny room open," I admitted.

"And all the bunnies ran out!" Max said.

"But all the bunnies are in their pen," Lauren said. "Except for Pixie. And she's here with you."

"We found all the bunnies," Max said. "And put them back into the pen."

"And that wasn't easy! They were all over the zoo," I added.

"Pixie was the only bunny we couldn't find," Max said. "Until Michelle thought to look in the supply closet."

"And then we got locked in!" I finished.

"I can't believe you found the bunnies and put them back," Lauren said. "And all by yourselves! But you shouldn't have tried to do such a big job like scrubbing the bunny pen. Not alone."

"I would have helped you clean out the bunny pen," my dad piped in. "I know about this great cleanser. It's very mild but so powerful!"

"My dad *does* know a lot about cleaning," I said with a smile. Then I remembered something. I nudged Max. "Tell Lauren about the frog!" I whispered.

"Oh, yeah," Max said.

"The frog?" Mrs. Wade asked. "What frog?"

Max pointed to the glass tank on the

shelf in the closet. The frog looked at everyone with its big bulging eyes.

"This frog," Max explained. "I found him in the garden when we were looking for bunnies. Isn't he great?"

"He is cute," Lauren said. She looked into the tank. "Would you like to help me set up a nice home for him?"

Max grinned. "Okay!"

My dad gave me another hug. "I'm just glad you're safe, Michelle."

I hugged him back. "I'm glad Pixie is safe!"

"Pixie!" Max exclaimed. "We have to show them her trick!"

"Yeah!" I grabbed the bunny treats. "Let's do it!"

Max put Pixie on one side of the broomstick. I knelt on the other side.

"Jump for the treat, Pixie!" I waved a treat in front of her nose.

"You can do it!" Max said.

Pixie's nose twitched. She smelled the treat. Then she leaped off the floor—and over the broomstick!

Everyone cheered as I fed Pixie her treat.

"That's incredible!" Mr. Wade said.

My dad clapped. "Way to go, kids!"

"I am very impressed," Lauren said. "It looks like we've got the zoo's official Easter Bunny right here!"

Max and I screamed. We both jumped up and down.

"We did it, Michelle," Max said.

"Thanks, Max," I said. "Pixie couldn't have done it without you. And neither could I!"

"Let's go!" Lauren said. "We're missing the party." She picked up Pixie and carried her out.

"Everyone is waiting for you," Dad told

me. "Uncle Jesse and Aunt Becky brought Alex and Nicky. You've got to help them find Easter eggs. And I know you want to find some for yourself. After all, you worked so hard on all this."

We walked outside together. White fluffy clouds floated by in the blue sky.

They looked like a bunch of bunnies to me!

"I'm glad we didn't miss the whole party," Max said.

"Me too," I agreed.

Now that all the bunnies were safe and sound, Max and I could have some fun! We were partners in the egg toss. Later we did a dance called the bunny hop with Gracie and Manuel. Then we got our cheeks decorated by a face painter. We even helped Alex and Nicky hunt for Easter eggs. And we found a few for ourselves too.

"It feels like we're looking for bunnies all over again!" Max laughed.

The twins ran back to the picnic tables to show Uncle Jesse and Aunt Becky their basket of eggs. Max and I followed them. Soon the zoo's official Easter Bunny would be announced!

Julia came up to us. "I heard you two got locked in the supply closet. Were you hiding just like your dopey bunny?" she said and laughed.

Max and I looked at each other and smiled. Julia wouldn't be laughing for long!

Then Lauren began speaking into a microphone. "Thank you all for coming out today," she said. "I have an announcement to make. Each year Old MacDonald's Petting Zoo picks a very special rabbit to be the official Easter Bunny. And this year it's . . . Pixie!" She held up the shy little bunny.

Everyone oohed and ahhed, of course. After all, Pixie *was* the cutest bunny!

"Not fair!" Julia frowned. "Mr. Fluffy should be the Easter Bunny! I want to talk to the judges!" she said and stormed off.

Max and I laughed. Julia will never change. Then I realized that the party would be over soon. And there was one more thing we had to do before we went home.

"Let's go say good-bye to the bunnies," I said to Max.

"Okay," Max agreed.

We found Max's mom and dad by the bunny pen.

Mr. Wade smiled when he saw his son. "I'm so happy with all the hard work you've put into this, Max. You've done a great job!"

Max's face lit up. "Thanks, Dad!"

"Your mom and I have agreed to let you

adopt a bunny," Mr. Wade said. "You've earned it!"

I wanted to jump up and down with joy. Max had done it!

Finally, Funny for Bunnies was getting a bunny!

But Max said something surprising.

"Um, no, thanks," he said. "I don't want a bunny anymore. They're too much work. I want a frog. Frogs are cool!"

Mr. Wade nodded. "Okay. We'll talk to Lauren about it."

"I can't believe it. All that work, and now you want a *frog*?" I said to Max.

Max shrugged. "I think I'll be much happier with a frog," he said, but then he frowned.

"What's the matter, Max?" I asked. "Did you change your mind again?"

"No." Max shook his head. "It's just that I had a name all picked out—for when I got a rabbit. Now that I'm getting a frog, I don't know what to call it. Do you have any ideas?"

I grinned. "You bet I do!" I didn't even have to think about this one. "Call it Bunny!" I said. "And that's my advice!"

Hi, I'm Michelle Tanner!

I write the advice column for my school newspaper, the Third-Grade Buzz. I get a lot of letters, and I answer them in my column. But sometimes it's just hard to get started. Sometimes you just don't know what to say! That's why I came up with my handy-dandy instant letter. It will give you some tips on what to put in your letter. So turn the page and check it out!

An instant letter is fun and easy. Just check off the replies or fill in your own answers where I've left space.

_____
(put date here)

Dear_____
(put friend's name here)

(1) Hi! How are you?

(2) I had a lot of fun over spring break. Right before writing this letter, I

___ read the best book of my life!

___ pretended to be a monkey at the zoo.

___ _____
(fill in your own answer)

_____

_____

Tomorrow I am going to

___ visit my favorite cousins.

___ eat seventeen jelly sandwiches.

___ _____
(fill in your own answer)

_____

_____

(3) What have you been up to?

(4) My parents said that I could get a

_____
(fill in the blank)

I get to pick it out all by myself!
I was thinking of getting

____ a puppy.

____ a chemistry set.

____ (fill in your own answer)

_____

_____

(5) Well, I guess I'd better be going. I have to

____ set the table.

____ tell my mom I want candy for dinner.

____ (fill in your own answer)

_____

_____

(6) See ya!

Sincerely,

_____
(sign your name here)

Here are some ideas to get you started just in case you get stuck.

(1) Say hi and ask how your friend is doing.

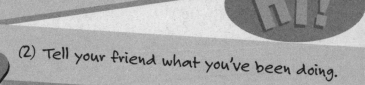

(2) Tell your friend what you've been doing.

(3) Ask your friend what he or she has been up to.

(4) Talk about something you care about.

(5) Say good-bye!

Do you need some advice—or want to ask me a question? I may be able to answer you in one of my future columns! I wish I could answer all of your letters, but I get too many! I would still love to hear from you. Write to me, Michelle, at:

Dear Michelle
c/o HarperEntertainment
10 East 53rd Street
New York, NY 10022

You can use the cool postcard in this book. It already has the address on it!

Check out these other great

titles